Dirty Bertie

CRACKERS!

To Mrs Burns (the real Bertie's mum) and
all at Bishop Martin Primary School ~ D R
To the children of Radcliffe on Trent
Junior School ~ A M

STRIPES PUBLISHING
An imprint of Little Tiger Press
1 The Coda Centre, 189 Munster Road,
London SW6 6AW

A paperback original
First published in Great Britain in 2008

Characters created by David Roberts
Text copyright © Alan MacDonald, 2008
Illustrations copyright © David Roberts, 2008

ISBN: 978-1-84715-048-6

The right of Alan MacDonald and David Roberts to
be identified as the author and illustrator of this work
respectively has been asserted by them in accordance
with the Copyright, Designs and Patents Act, 1988.

Printed and bound in the UK.
10 9 8 7 6

Dirty Bertie

CRACKERS!

DAVID ROBERTS WRITTEN BY ALAN MACDONALD

Stripes

Collect all the
Dirty Bertie books!

Contents

BAAA!

CHAPTER 1

Bertie burst into the kitchen.

"Ahaarr, shipmates!" he cried.

He was wearing his pirate hat and eyepatch, and brandishing a cutlass.

"Bertie, please don't wave that in here," said Mum wearily.

"I'm practising," Bertie explained. "It's the auditions for the Christmas play today."

Dirty Bertie

Every year, the school's Christmas concert took place at St Wilfrid's Church. There were readings and carols, but the highlight was always the play. Bertie had never been chosen for one of the main parts, but this year things were going to be different.

"I thought it was a nativity play," said Mum.

"It is," said Bertie. "I'm going to be one of the three kings."

"Dressed like that?"

"I'm the pirate king," said Bertie.

Mum rolled her eyes. "Bertie, there aren't any pirates in the Christmas story."

"I know, but there could be. Instead of just following a star there could be a big battle between the pirates and the robbers."

"What robbers?"

"The ones fighting the pirates," replied Bertie.

"Bertie, you can't just change the story any way you like!"

"Why not?" asked Bertie. "Everyone's seen it before."

"In any case," said Mum, "if Miss Boot sees you dressed like that you probably won't get a part at all."

"Miss Boot isn't doing the play this year," replied Bertie. "It's Miss Darling."

Dirty Bertie

Miss Darling was new to Bertie's school, which explained why she'd agreed to direct the play. Every other teacher in the school avoided it like the plague.

"Children, children!" she said, clapping her hands together. "Let's make a start, shall we? Now, who would like to audition first?"

A dozen hands shot into the air. Miss Darling chose the boy wearing a black eyepatch.

"And you are?"

"Bertie," said Bertie.

"Well, Bertie, perhaps you could take off your hat first."

"It's my costume," said Bertie.

"That's lovely, but this story hasn't got any pirates. It's about the baby Jesus being born in the manger."

"It's got three kings," said Bertie.

"Yes, that's right."

"Well, I'm the pirate king."

Miss Darling ran a hand through her hair. "Why don't you just read the part and we'll see how we get on, shall we?"

Bertie clumped across the stage. He swished his cutlass through the air.

"Ahaarr!" he said in his best pirate accent. "We be three kings and we be following the star…"

Miss Darling held up a hand to stop him. "Perhaps it would work better without the funny voice."

Bertie frowned. "That's how pirates talk," he said. "It's not meant to be funny."

"I know," said Miss Darling. "But could you just try it in your own voice. Please."

Bertie clomped off stage – and clomped back on. "We are three kings and we're following the star…"

He swished his sword a bit too wildly.

"Ow!" cried a voice. "You nearly poked me in the eye!"

It was Bertie's sworn enemy, Know-All Nick.

"It's not my fault," said Bertie. "How am

I supposed to act with you in the way?"

He gave Nick a shove. Nick shoved him back, knocking off Bertie's hat. Bertie raised his cutlass.

"MISS! Bertie's fighting!" whined Nick.

"I think that will do, Bertie. Come and sit down," said Miss Darling.

Bertie sat down. On the whole he felt the audition had gone pretty well. He was bound to get the part of the pirate king. After all, he was the only one who had bothered to come in costume.

CHAPTER 2

The following day, Miss Darling gave out the parts. Bertie waited eagerly to hear his name.

"Josh, Zadie and Nicholas, you will be the kings. I'm sure you'll all be wonderful."

Bertie couldn't believe it. Know-All Nick – a king? He didn't even have his own eyepatch!

Dirty Bertie

Nick slunk over to Bertie.

"What part did you get, Bertie?"

"A shepherd."

"Only a shepherd? Poor you!"

"Better than a smelly old king," said Bertie.

"How many lines have you got?"

Bertie shrugged. "I haven't looked yet."

"I have," said Nick. "You've got one – on page 15. I've got hundreds. Look, I'm on nearly every page."

He thrust his script under Bertie's nose.

Bertie ignored him.

Dirty Bertie

"And Miss Darling wants me to sing a solo," Nick went on. "She says I sing beautifully."

"Shame your face is so ugly," Bertie replied.

Rehearsals got under way. Nick wore a purple cloak. His gold crown glittered

with jewels. Bertie wore a tea towel that flopped in his eyes.

"Now," said Miss Darling. "It is night. All is calm, all is bright. Angels, tiptoe in and gather round the stable. Kings, lay your gifts by the manger. Shepherds … where are the shepherds?"

Bertie's head popped out from behind the curtain. "Sorry, Miss, we've lost one of the sheep."

Miss Darling frowned. "You don't have any sheep."

"They're pretend sheep," said Bertie. "I counted six but now there's only five."

"Never mind, just bring them in and gather round the manger."

Bertie, Darren and Eugene clumped across the stage, making loud "baa-ing" noises. There was a bit of shoving between the kings and the shepherds, who all wanted to be at the front. Miss Darling waited for them to settle.

"Now, the lights dim and Nicholas comes to the front," she said.

Nick gave Bertie a gloating smile. He stepped forward and took a deep breath.

"Silent night, holeeee night!"

"Beautiful!" sighed Miss Darling, clasping her hands.

"All is calm, all is bright…"

"BAAA!"

"Who is doing that?" cried Miss Darling.

Zadie raised her hand. "Please, Miss, it's Bertie!"

"Bertie!" said Miss Darling.

"Sorry, Miss, it's our lost sheep," said Bertie. "He's come back."

Know-All Nick glared at him and began again.

"Silent night, holy ni—"

"I know, Miss!" It was Bertie again.

"What is it now?" sighed Miss Darling.

"What if we had a sheepdog?"

"You mean a pretend dog?"

"No, a real one," said Bertie. "He could round up the sheep."

"That's a lovely idea, Bertie, but we don't have a sheepdog."

"My dog Whiffer could do it," said Bertie.

"Brilliant!" said Darren.

"Wicked!" said Eugene.

Miss Darling looked flustered. "I'm not sure it's such a good idea. You can't bring a dog into church."

"Why not?" asked Bertie.

"Because … well … what if he misbehaves?"

"He won't, Miss. Whiffer's been to dog-training classes. He's got a certificate."

"Even so…" Miss Darling looked doubtful.

"Please, Miss!" begged Bertie. "He'd be brilliant."

Miss Darling hesitated. "Why don't I think about it?" she said.

"Great!" said Bertie.

CHAPTER 3

With so much to do, Miss Darling soon forgot about Bertie's idea. But Bertie didn't forget. In his mind, the matter was settled. If Miss Darling hadn't actually said "No", she must have meant "Yes".

On the night of the play Bertie got to the church early. He was dressed in a tea towel and his old checked dressing gown.

Dirty Bertie

Whiffer was at his side. Bertie hadn't
asked Mum or Dad if Whiffer could be in
the play — he wanted it to be a surprise.

Miss Boot got a bit of a surprise, too.
As she came into the vestry, she almost
fell over Whiffer.

"SHOO!" she screeched. "GET AWAY
FROM ME, YOU BRUTE!"

"It's only Whiffer, Miss. He won't hurt
you," said Bertie.

Miss Boot turned very pale.
She didn't seem to like dogs.
She was flattened against
the wall as if she
thought Whiffer was
going to eat her.

"Bertie! Get him out
of here!" she
squawked.

Dirty Bertie

"But he's in the play." Whiffer wagged his tail and barked excitedly.

Miss Boot began to shake. "Don't be ridiculous!" she said. "Now shoo!"

"But he is, Miss, honestly! Miss Darling said. Didn't you, Miss?"

Miss Boot turned on Miss Darling, who was pinning up the hem of Mary's dress.

"Oh dear, I think perhaps there's been a misunderstanding," said Miss Darling. "Bertie did ask if he could bring his dog, but I said…"

"I don't care what you said!" snapped Miss Boot. "It's out of the question. I won't have a dog ruining the performance. Now take him home."

At that moment, there was a knock on the door and the vicar poked his head into the room.

"Everybody ready?" he asked, beaming.
"The audience are all in."

"Oh dear!" said Miss Darling, staring at
Whiffer. "I'm sure he'll behave himself."

Miss Boot glared at Bertie. "He better.
If that dog so much as whimpers, I will
hold you personally responsible, Bertie.
Do I make myself clear?"

Dirty Bertie

Bertie's mum and dad had seats in the front row.

The play began. Know-All Nick entered wearing his gold crown and spied the star in the east through his telescope. The junior choir then sang *Little Donkey* while Mary and Joseph plodded around the church on the way to Bethlehem.

Finally came the entrance of the shepherds.

Darren, Eugene and Bertie clomped on to the stage holding their crooks and peering out from under their tea towels.

Dad turned pale when he saw who was with them. "Good grief!" he hissed. "Isn't that Whiffer?"

"It can't be!" said Mum.

"It is!" whispered Dad. "What's he doing here? I thought he was at home."

"Bertie didn't mention anything!"

"No," said Dad, grimly. "I bet he didn't."

They watched nervously as Whiffer crossed the stage and sniffed around the choir stalls. They waited for him to growl or bark or do something disgusting on the floor. But Whiffer behaved as if he'd been acting all his life. When Bertie sat, he sat, too, and rested his head in Bertie's lap.

"Ahhhhhhh!" went the audience.

From that moment on, Whiffer was the star of the play. He followed the shepherds on the road to Bethlehem and wagged his tail when the innkeeper patted his head. Children in the audience laughed. Parents smiled. Even Miss Boot stopped frowning.

Everything went perfectly until the final scene. The angels tiptoed on, the

kings laid their gifts at the manger, the
shepherds knelt and Whiffer lay down
beside Bertie. Miss Boot dimmed the
lights low and Miss Darling plink-plonked
on the piano. It was Know-All Nick's big
moment.

"Silent night, holeeee night!" he sang.

Whiffer pricked up his ears.

"All is calm, all is bright…"

"OWWWW! OWWWWW!" howled Whiffer, joining in the song.

Bertie put a hand over his muzzle and tried to silence him, but that only brought giggles from the audience.

"Keep going!" whispered Miss Darling. "Keep going!" She plinked the opening bars again.

"Silent night, holeeee night," sang Nick. "All is calm…"

"OWWWW! OWWWWW! OWWWWWW!" bayed Whiffer, throwing back his head.

The audience shook with laughter. Nick bellowed louder.

"SILENT NIGHT…!"

Dirty Bertie

Whiffer howled louder still. Nick lost his temper and hurled his gift at Whiffer's head. It missed and bounced off Bertie's.

"Ow!" he said, loudly.

Bertie pushed Nick in the back with his crook.

"ARGHHH!" Nick stumbled forwards, and fell into the front row of the audience. He clambered back on stage, crimson with fury.

Dirty Bertie

"GET THEM!" he yelled.

"GET THEM!" Bertie yelled back.

The kings charged the shepherds.

The shepherds charged the kings.

Crowns were trampled underfoot. Tea towels were torn. Whiffer bounded around the stage, barking joyfully. Bertie caught sight of Miss Boot's face as he ducked a flying sandal. She looked like she was about to explode.

CHAPTER 4

"A disaster!" sighed Miss Darling.

"Never again!" vowed Miss Skinner.

The audience were leaving the church and making their way home. Bertie felt it might be a good time for him to slip away, too. But he would have to get past Miss Boot, who was standing at the door. He pulled his tea towel over his eyes and tried to mingle with the crowd.

"BERTIE!" boomed Miss Boot. "I want a word with you."

Bertie backed away. "It wasn't my fault…" he stammered. "How was I to know Whiffer doesn't like Nick's singing?"

"I warned you," stormed Miss Boot. "I warned you if that—"

She broke off. Whiffer had trotted over to say hello. Miss Boot backed off. Her face had gone white.

"Shoo! Get away!" she said.

"It's OK. He won't bite, he just wants to play!" said Bertie.

But Miss Boot didn't want to play. Miss Boot was in retreat. Whiffer bounded after her. With a squawk, Miss Boot bolted into the vestry and slammed the door behind her.

Dirty Bertie

"Miss Boot?" said Bertie, through the door.

"GO AWAY!" shouted Miss Boot. "JUST GO!"

Bertie didn't need any more persuasion. He went.

Darren and Eugene were waiting outside.

"Well, what happened?" asked Eugene.

"Nothing," said Bertie. "She told me to go."

"Teachers!" said Darren, shaking his head.

"Anyway," said Eugene, brightening up, "tomorrow's the Christmas holidays. What shall we do?"

Bertie considered it. "I know!" he said. "We could take Whiffer carol singing!"

Dirty Bertie

"Brilliant!" said Darren.

"Wicked!" said Eugene.

"I'm sure Miss Boot would love a visit," said Bertie. "Anyone know where she lives?"

ELF!

CHAPTER 1

Bertie could hardly wait. Tomorrow was the school Christmas Fair. Mince pies and sticky fudge. Jam jars stuffed with sweets. Tombola, Lucky Dip and Guess the Weight of the Christmas Pudding. Maybe Miss Boot would fall off the stage like last year?

"HO HO HO! MERRY CHRISTMAS!" boomed a voice.

Bertie looked up. His dad was wearing a bright-red suit, black boots and a cotton-wool beard.

"Well, what do you think?" he asked.

"Who are you meant to be?" asked Bertie.

"Who does it look like? I'm Father Christmas!"

"Oh," said Bertie.

"It's for the fair. Santa's Grotto. Mr Grouch can't do it this year as he's lost his voice, so I offered to stand in."

"You're going to be Father Christmas?" said Bertie.

"Yes."

"At the fair? *My* school fair?"

"Yes. In fact I was wondering if you might like to help?"

"Me?" said Bertie. "How?"

Dirty Bertie

When parents asked for help they usually meant laying the table or weeding the garden. They never wanted help finishing a box of chocolates.

Dad held up a costume. It was a little red tunic with a green felt hat.

"I need an elf," he said. "To help in the grotto."

"Oh," said Bertie. "No thanks."

"Go on, Bertie, it'll be fun."

Bertie shook his head. No way was he going to dress up in a soppy pixie outfit and have everyone laugh at him.

"You won't have to do much," said Dad. "Just take the money and show the children in."

"Why can't you do it?"

"Because I'm Father Christmas. I'll be busy in the grotto."

"Well I'll be busy, too," said Bertie.

"Doing what?"

"Going round the fair."

"There'll be plenty of time to do that afterwards," argued Dad.

"Sorry," said Bertie.

Dad pulled off his beard and sighed. "Oh well, I'll just have to give the present to someone else then."

Bertie pricked up his ears. "What present?"

"The one I was going to give you from my sack. I've got hundreds. Help me tomorrow and you can take your pick."

Bertie considered it for a second. He loved getting presents and with a whole sackful to choose from, there was bound to be something good.

"OK," he said. "I'll do it. Can I have the present now?"

Dad shook his head. "Oh no. First you help at the fair, then you get the present."

Dirty Bertie

Bertie waited till he heard his dad tip-
tapping on the computer, then crept
upstairs. Now where would Dad have
hidden a whopping big sack of presents?
Bertie sneaked into his parents' room
and began to rummage through drawers.
Ahaa! His eyes fell on something hidden
under the bed. Father Christmas's
present sack. He dragged it out. The sack
was bulging with presents, each wrapped
in gold paper. Bertie gazed at them
longingly. Surely no one would know if he
just took a little peep at one?

RIPPP! Whoops! A bit of wrapping
paper came off in his hand. Bertie peered
through the hole he'd made. Inside was
a Fairy Trixabelle Magic Wand. Yuck!

Dirty Bertie

He'd rather have a bucket of slugs.
He tossed the present aside.

RIP! A jigsaw.

RIP! A set of felt pens.

RIP! Wait a moment… Bertie
glimpsed something smooth and shiny
silver. It couldn't be… It was! An Alien
Egg from the Planet Slimos! Bertie had
been begging his
parents to buy him
an Alien Egg for
weeks. Darren had
got one for his
birthday. When
you dunked the egg
in water, out flopped a
squidgy little alien in
a sea of green
gloop.

Dirty Bertie

Bertie thought quickly. Maybe he could just take the egg now and hide it in his bedroom? No, too risky. Mum was always sneaking into his room to tidy up. There was nothing else for it, he'd have to wait till tomorrow and claim the egg as his reward. But what if some greedy child got there first and stole his present?

Suddenly Bertie had a brainwave. Taking a felt pen, he made a big red blob on the wrapping paper. Now he'd be able to tell it apart from all the other presents. He stuck down the torn wrapping paper with Sellotape and slipped the present back into the sack. That Alien Egg was as good as his.

CHAPTER 2

"Why do I have to wear this stupid dress?" moaned Bertie.

"It's not a dress, it's an elf costume," said Dad.

"Can't I be a goblin?"

"No! Father Christmas doesn't have goblins."

Dad was struggling into his costume.

Dirty Bertie

The Christmas Fair had just opened and people were already streaming into the hall. Bertie pulled back a curtain and gazed longingly at the stalls.

"Couldn't I just have a quick look round?" he begged.

"Bertie, we've been over this! Just try and be helpful."

"I *am* being helpful!"

Bertie perched on his stool, miserably.

 His tights were too tight and the pointed hat made him look like Noddy. He hoped Darren and Eugene didn't see him dressed like this. They'd be giggling about it for weeks.

Dirty Bertie

Santa's Grotto had been set up on the stage behind a curtain. The entrance was two screens draped with tinsel and fairy lights. Father Christmas sat waiting with the sack of presents by his side. It was Bertie who'd suggested putting a small pile of presents on the floor. He'd made sure the Alien Egg was on top where he could keep an eye on it.

A queue of small, excited children waited outside. Bertie poked his head out.

"Are you an elf?" asked a little boy.

"No, I'm a goblin," scowled Bertie.

"Where's Father Christmas?"

"He's in there," said Bertie. "It's fifty pence."

The boy handed over his money. Bertie dropped it into a tin and pulled back the curtain.

"You can pick any present from the sack," he explained. "But don't touch the ones on the floor."

"Why not?" asked the boy.

"Because they belong to the goblins."

"Oh."

"And if you take one the goblins will find out. And they'll come looking for you – in the night."

"Eeek!" The boy gave a frightened cry and dashed into the grotto.

"HO HO HO! MERRY CHRISTMAS!" boomed Father Christmas.

This is easy, thought Bertie. No one was going to get their hands on his Alien Egg.

CHAPTER 3

Rumble, rumble went the tombola stall.
Bertie peeped out through the curtains.
He watched Know-All Nick come away
from the Lucky Dip, clutching a prize.
Eugene and Darren were queuing at the
Treasure Hunt stall. Everyone was having
a great time except him. It wasn't fair.
He was stuck in Santa's grotty grotto all

afternoon and the queue of children showed no sign of coming to an end.

"Hello, Bertie!" piped a high voice.

It was Angela Nicely with her friend Laura. Angela lived next door and had been in love with Bertie ever since her first day at school. Bertie did his best to avoid her.

"You do look funny, Bertie!" she giggled. "Are you Robbing Hood?"

"I'm a goblin," scowled Bertie.

"Can I have a go of your hat?"

"No," said Bertie. "Only goblins can wear them."

"I won a prize," boasted Angela, licking a lollipop. "I won it on the Lucky Dip. Have you won a prize?"

"No," said Bertie. "I haven't been on the Lucky Dip. I haven't been on anything."

"Oh, poor Bertie," cooed Angela, patting his hand fondly.

Bertie pulled his hand away quickly. He'd had an idea.

"Anyway, who wants to go round boring old stalls?" he said. "Being a goblin's much more fun."

"Is it?" asked Angela.

"Of course," said Bertie. "Especially if you're the Head Goblin and you get to guard all this money."

"Gosh!" said Angela, staring at the large pile of coins in the tin.

"*And* I'm in charge of the presents."

Angela's eyes widened. "The presents?"

"Yes. No one's allowed to touch them, except me and Father Christmas."

Angela and Laura were looking at him with new respect.

"Can I be a goblin, too?" begged Angela.

"And me?" said Laura.

"No," said Bertie. "You're not old enough."

"Please, Bertie."

"Sorry."

"*Pleeeeease!*"

"Oh all right," said Bertie. "You sit here."

Angela climbed on to the stool and Bertie put his pixie hat on her head.

"Now you're the Head Goblin," he said.

"Am I?" beamed Angela, proudly.

"Yes, and you've got to take everyone's money."

"What do I do?" demanded Laura.

"You can, er … make sure people go in one at a time."

"But what are you going to do, Bertie?"

"I'm, um, just going to pop out for a bit and check round the fair," said Bertie. "You sit there and take the money till I get back. Oh, and make sure you tell people they can only have presents from the sack, not the ones on the floor."

"Why not?" asked Angela.

"'Cos they belong to the goblins."

"I'm a goblin," beamed Angela. "I'm the Head Goblin."

"Yes," said Bertie, "but you mustn't touch those presents."

"Why not?"

"Because I'm in charge and I say so," said Bertie.

He slipped out before Angela could ask any more questions.

CHAPTER 4

At last he was free! Adoring Angela could take care of Santa's Grotto while he had a chance to enjoy the fair. After all, he'd slaved for hours taking people's money, he deserved a little time off.

Bertie had a brilliant time going round all the stalls. He bought a bag of fudge, won a Glo Glo Yo-Yo at the Lucky Dip

and guessed the weight of the Giant
Christmas Pudding (a ton). In fact he
enjoyed himself so much that by the
time he returned, Santa's Grotto was
starting to pack up.

Father Christmas didn't look pleased.

"Bertie! Where have you been?" he
snapped.

"Oh, um, I just popped out for a bit,"
Bertie said through a mouthful of fudge.

"I told you to stay on the door, not
walk off and abandon me."

"I didn't walk off," said Bertie. "I left
someone in charge."

"Yes, Angela Nicely and her friend.
They let everyone in for free."

"Did they?" Bertie was looking around
the grotto. The sack was empty and the
floor was bare.

Dirty Bertie

"Um, where are all the presents?" he asked, anxiously.

"Mmm? They've all gone. I saved you one, though I can't say you deserve it."

Bertie grabbed the present from his dad. He turned it over looking for a red blob. There wasn't one.

"Where is it?" he gasped.

"Where's what?"

"The present that was right there – on top of the pile!"

"Oh, I gave it to one of the girls," said Dad. "They were very insistent. They didn't want presents from my sack – only the 'special goblin ones' on the floor."

"NO!" cried Bertie.

"What's the matter? Where are you off to now?"

Bertie rushed out. He had to find Angela before it was too late. There was no sign of her in the hall. Or in the corridor. Outside, he spotted her in the playground with her mum. A present was tucked under her arm.

"Hello, Bertie!" she trilled, as he dashed towards her.

"I need that back … there's been a mistake," panted Bertie. "I'll swap it for this one."

"No thanks," smiled Angela.

"This one's much better."

"I like this one. Father Christmas gave it to me."

Bertie felt in his pocket. "I'll give you fifty pence for it," he offered.

Angela shook her head.

"Fifty pence and a bag of fudge. There's two bits left."

"No thanks." Angela eyed his Lucky Dip prize. "But I haven't got a yo-yo…"

Dirty Bertie

Angela walked off happily down the road, clutching her winnings. Bertie breathed a sigh of relief. It had been a close run thing, but he finally had it. An Alien Egg of his very own. He couldn't wait to get it home and dunk it in water.

He checked the wrapping paper. No red blob. He turned the present over. The paper had been neatly opened at one end, but still no red blob. Surely it wasn't … it couldn't be… Bertie tore off the wrapping. Inside was a Fairy Trixabelle Magic Wand.

Dirty Bertie

"ANGELA!" yelled Bertie.

Angela turned and waved to him as she tripped off down the road chatting to Laura. Bertie caught sight of something in Laura's hands – something smooth and round and silver. Even from that distance, he knew exactly what it was…

CRACKERS!

CHAPTER 1

"Oh no!" said Mum, putting down the phone. "Great-Aunt Morag's coming for Christmas!"

"You're joking!" said Dad.

"I wish I was," sighed Mum. "She's arriving on Christmas Eve."

Dad groaned. Suzy rolled her eyes. Bertie's mouth fell open and a piece of

toast plopped on to the table. He
licked it up quickly before anyone noticed.

"What about Aunt June?" said Dad.
"Great-Aunt Morag always stays with
her."

"Aunt June's got a bad back," said
Mum.

"Uncle Ed then?"

Mum shook her head. "He's taken
Gran on a cruise."

"There must be someone who can
have her!"

"There isn't! They're either away or
sick."

"Can't you say that we're sick?"
suggested Bertie.

"We're not, are we, Bertie?"

"We will be if she comes," said Bertie.
"We'll be sick of the sight of her."

Dirty Bertie

Bertie stared glumly at his plate. It wasn't fair. He'd been looking forward to Christmas for weeks and now it was going to be  ruined. They might as well cancel it.

Great-Aunt Morag was about a hundred years old and gloomier than a wet Monday morning. Last time she came to stay she'd grumbled and griped about everything. She was mean, too. Dad said that she had a padlock on her purse. Other uncles and aunts slipped ten pound notes into your Christmas card, but not Mean Aunt Morag.

Dirty Bertie

"Well, she's not sleeping in my room," said Suzy.

"She'll have to," replied Mum. "Bertie's room is such a mess."

"But where am I going to sleep?"

"On the camp bed in Bertie's room."

"NO!" cried Suzy. "His room smells!"

"You're the one who smells," said Bertie.

"You are!"

"You are!"

Dirty Bertie

"Enough!" cried Mum. "Great-Aunt Morag is coming and we'll have to make the best of it. So you better start thinking what you can buy her for Christmas."

"Why?" said Bertie. "She never gets me anything."

"Nonsense, she sent you a present last year."

"Huh!" scoffed Bertie. "Call that a present!"

Mean Aunt Morag had sent him a Birds of Britain bookmark. It had the twenty pence price label stuck to the back.

"Anyway," said Mum, "it doesn't have to be expensive. It's the thought that counts."

Bertie sighed deeply. Christmas was only a few days away and he still hadn't bought presents for any of his family.

Dirty Bertie

Now he had Mean Aunt Morag to think about, too. And there was another problem – the last time he looked he only had fifty pence in his piggy bank.

Next day, Bertie trailed around the shops after his mum, looking for presents. But unless you liked paper clips, there wasn't much you could buy for fifty pence. He was about to give up when he spotted something in the newsagent's window. It was a box of shiny red crackers. Bertie loved crackers. He loved the presents, the jokes, the party hats, and the loud bang they made when you pulled them. The only problem was the box of crackers cost a lot more than fifty pence.

Dirty Bertie

Bertie pressed his nose to the window. Suddenly a brilliant brainwave came to him. Why pay for crackers when he could easily make his own? After all, his mum said it was the thought that counts – and Bertie had thought of this all by himself.

CHAPTER 2

Back in his bedroom Bertie fished out his book of *101 Crafty Things to Make*. He found "Crackers" on page 48. It looked dead easy. All you needed was glue, ribbon, coloured paper and a bunch of toilet roll tubes.

Bertie set to work. He spilled quite a lot of glue and one of the crackers stuck

to the carpet, but otherwise he was
pretty pleased with the results. Soon he
had five fat, sticky, orange crackers. Now
for the things to go inside. The party hats
didn't take long – Bertie was super
speedy at cutting out. And he knew
millions of brilliant cracker jokes. He
wrote them on scraps of paper…

WHAT DO YOU CALL A PIRATE
WEARING PANTS?

Long Johns Silver!

HOW DO YOU MAKE A TISSUE DANCE?

Put a boogie in it!

WHAT'S THE DIFFERENCE
BETWEEN A SCHOOL DINNER AND
A PILE OF POO?

School dinner comes on a plate!

Into the crackers they went. All he
needed now was a few presents. Wait a
moment – what
about all the stuff he
kept in his Top
Secret box? Bertie
dragged it out from under the bed.
Perfect! There were tons of things in
here that he'd love to get in a cracker.
His family were so lucky. Even Mean
Aunt Morag might crack a smile.

DING DONG! Great-Aunt Morag was
at the door.

"Hello! How lovely to see you," said
Mum, cheerily. "How was your journey?"

"Long," scowled Great-Aunt Morag.
"And tiring. I've got a dreadful headache."

"Well, you're here now," said Mum. "The children have been so looking forward to seeing you."

"Yes," said Bertie. "When are you going?"

"Bertie," said Mum quickly, "why don't you take Great-Aunt Morag's bag up to her room? I hope you're hungry, I've saved you some supper."

"Humph. What is it?"

"Pasta."

"I don't like pasta. It gives me wind," said Great-Aunt Morag. "I'd like some vegetable soup – and not too hot."

They all sat round the table while Great-Aunt Morag slurped her way through her soup. Afterwards, she sat in the lounge and grumbled about the weather, the trains and the expense of Christmas.

"Well," she said at last. "Time for bed."

"What?" said Bertie.

Mum glanced at the clock. "It is nine o'clock."

"But we're allowed to stay up on Christmas Eve!" begged Bertie.

Great-Aunt Morag clicked her tongue. "Children these days stay up far too late."

Dirty Bertie

"But can't we play a game?" asked Bertie.

"Certainly not. Games are noisy."

"Or watch a film."

"I don't like films."

"But … it's Christmas Eve," wailed Bertie. "I want to wait up for Father Christmas!"

Great-Aunt Morag looked down her nose. "Father Christmas doesn't come to naughty children," she said. "Good children go to bed when they are told."

Bertie plodded upstairs to bed. This was going to be the worst Christmas ever.

CHAPTER 3

Bertie shot out of bed. It was Christmas Day! He almost tripped over Suzy in his haste to get to the door.

Downstairs he peeped into the lounge. Yesssss! His stocking was bulging with presents. But where was everybody?

"Wake up!" cried Bertie, rushing into

his parents' room and jumping on to
the bed.

Mum rubbed her eyes.

"Urrrrgh! What time is it?"

"Present time!" shouted Bertie. "Can
I open my presents?"

Mum squinted at her alarm clock.

"Bertie! It's five o'clock in the morning!"

"Is it? Can I open my presents?"

"No, go back to bed! And I don't want
to hear another peep from you until
after seven."

Bertie stomped back to his room.
He stared at his alarm clock. TICK, TICK,
TICK. Why did they make clocks that
went so slow? The minutes crept by at a
snail's pace.

At last, the hands
ticked round to seven.

Dirty Bertie

"Time to get up!" yelled Bertie, bursting in on his parents again. "Can I open my presents now?"

Dad groaned. Mum sat up in bed.

"All right. Is Great-Aunt Morag awake?"

Bertie had forgotten all about his crabby aunt. He went to listen at her door and heard a rumbling snore coming from inside.

"She's asleep," he said.

"Well, we can't open presents without her. It would be rude," said Mum.

Dirty Bertie

"WHAT?" wailed Bertie. "But it's Christmas Day! Can't we wake her up?"

"NO, BERTIE!"

Suzy came in wearing her dressing gown. "Are we opening our presents?"

"No," said Bertie, dejectedly. "We've got to wait for Mean Aunt Morag."

Bertie paced up and down the kitchen, while his family ate breakfast. Eight o'clock went by. Nine. Half past nine. At this rate Christmas Day would be over.

"Can't we wake her up *now*?" begged Bertie.

"Maybe if someone took her up a cup of tea?" suggested Dad.

"I'll do it!" cried Bertie.

Luckily, there was still some lukewarm tea left in the teapot. Bertie sploshed some milk into a mug. He added a little tea and a few heaped spoonfuls of sugar. Then he dashed upstairs with it.

THUMP, THUMP, THUMP! He banged on the bedroom door.

"Who's that?" grunted his great-aunt.

"It's Bertie. I've brought you a cup of tea."

"Very well. Bring it in."

"Happy Christmas!" sang Bertie, handing her the cup.

Great-Aunt Morag was in her nightdress and hairnet. She looked like an ancient mummy.

Dirty Bertie

"Humph. Is it hot?" she demanded. "I don't like it too hot."

"Why don't you drink it downstairs?" suggested Bertie hopefully. "We're waiting to open our presents."

"Children today get far too many presents," grumbled Great-Aunt Morag. She took a gulp of tea and almost choked. "BLEEUGHH! It's stone cold!"

"Is it?" asked Bertie. "Sorry, it must've got cold while we were waiting for you."

CHAPTER 4

Bertie waited. Great-Aunt Morag got
washed and dressed, ate her breakfast
and went back upstairs to clean her
teeth. Finally, Bertie was allowed to open
his presents. He got a Beetle Bug board
game from Uncle Ed, £20 from Aunt
June and a pocket torch from Mean
Aunt Morag.

"It doesn't work!" he said.

"It needs batteries," said Great-Aunt Morag. "You'll have to save up."

Luckily, his gran had bought him something that did work. A Kings of Spin Stunt Car. Bertie couldn't wait to play with it.

BLEEP, BLEEP, BLEEP! WOO, WOO! CRUNCH!

It zoomed into the lounge and slammed into the TV stand, doing a somersault.

Mean Aunt Morag sucked in her breath. "I can feel my headache coming back," she moaned.

"Bertie," sighed Mum. "Turn it off."

Dirty Bertie

"But I've only just started playing with it," said Bertie.

"Can't you find something less noisy?"

"What about my Lazer Dazer Space Gun?"

"No, not in here."

"Can I watch TV then?"

Great-Aunt Morag tutted. "Children today watch far too much television."

"Maybe later," said Mum. "Why don't you sit quietly and read for a while?"

Bertie slumped on the sofa. What sort of Christmas was it if you couldn't even play with your toys or watch TV? He wished his mean old misery-guts aunt would go home. If she wanted peace and quiet why didn't she go and sit in a library? Or better still a graveyard; she might feel at home there.

Dirty Bertie

MERRY CHRISTMAS

Dirty Bertie

TICK, TICK, TICK. The minutes dragged
by in silence. Great-Aunt Morag's pen
scratched at her crossword.

"Is it lunchtime yet?" asked Dad,
hopefully.

"Not for an hour," replied Mum.

"I know," said Suzy. "We haven't had
Bertie's presents yet… Or did you
forget to buy any this year?"

"'Course I didn't," said Bertie,
brightening up. "I was saving mine for
lunchtime." He rushed upstairs to get
them.

At one o'clock Mum called everyone to
the table. Bertie had laid it himself and
next to each place was one of his
home-made crackers.

Dirty Bertie

"Ah, what could this be?" asked Dad, picking up a sticky lump.

"It's a cracker," said Bertie. "I made them myself. They've got presents and hats and everything."

"What a lovely idea, Bertie!" said Mum, delightedly. "They must have taken you ages."

Mean Aunt Morag wrinkled her nose.

"I hope they're not going to be noisy," she grumbled.

"No," said Bertie. "I couldn't find any bangs to put in them. But it's OK, I can shout when we pull them."

Everyone took hold of one end of a cracker and got ready to pull.

"One, two, three… BANG!" shouted Bertie.

The crackers came apart and Bertie's presents shot out over the table.

"Oh, good heavens!" said Mum. A set of Dracula dentures floated in her glass.

Dirty Bertie

"Eugh, gross!" said Suzy, staring at the plastic dog poo on her plate.

"Bertie!"
groaned Dad,
holding up a
severed finger,
dripping with
blood.

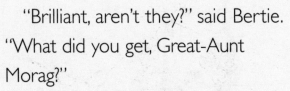

Dirty Bertie

"Brilliant, aren't they?" said Bertie. "What did you get, Great-Aunt Morag?"

Great-Aunt Morag mumbled something. She seemed to have her mouth full.

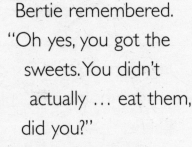

Bertie remembered. "Oh yes, you got the sweets. You didn't actually ... eat them, did you?"

Great-Aunt Morag's jaw stopped working. Her face turned white, then pink, then green. Her eyes bulged, her lips twitched. White froth bubbled at the corners of her mouth.

"ARGHHH! OOOH! URRRGGGH!" she cried, clutching at her throat and rushing from the room.

"You're not leaving already?" asked Mum. "What about Christmas dinner?"

Great-Aunt Morag carried her bag to the door. "If you think I'm staying to be insulted you are mistaken!" she fumed. "I am going home and I will not be coming back. Ever!"

WHAM! The door slammed shut.

Everyone turned to look at Bertie.

"Out of interest," said Dad, "what was in those sweets?"

Bertie gulped. "I think it might've said on the packet they were, um, soap sweets."

He got ready to run.

"Oh dear!" said Mum, smiling. "Poor Great-Aunt Morag! That was very bad of you, Bertie."

"Very bad," chuckled Dad. "Now then, who votes we eat Christmas dinner in front of the telly?"

Bertie whooped. It was going to be a cracking Christmas after all.

Out now: